Queen Victoria's Request

A story of grace and mercy

Charles Spurgeon
Illustrated by Jeff Anderson

Queen Victoria's Request, This edition: © 2008 Christian Focus Publications, Geanies House, Fearn, Tain, Ross-shire, IV20 1TW, Scotland, U.K. www.christianfocus.com. Printed in China.

CF4•K

Here is a story about an old ragged, dirty, beggar covered in coal dust who received a message from Her Most Gracious Majesty, Queen Victoria.

It read in this way: "You are hereby commanded to come, just as you are, to our palace at Windsor, to receive great and special favours at our hand. You will stay away at your peril."

SOAP
ONLY 2 p
BAR

The man read the message, and at first scarcely understood it; so he thought, "I must wash and prepare myself."

Then, he re-read the royal summons, and the words arrested him: "Come just as you are."

So he set off, and told all the people in the train where he was going and they laughed at him.

At length he arrived at Windsor Castle where he was stopped by the guard, and questioned. He explained why he had come, and showed the Queen's message so he was allowed to pass.

Next he met with a gentleman-in-waiting, who, after some explanations and expressions of astonishment, allowed him to enter the queen's apartments.

When there, the old beggar became frightened on account of his dirty and ragged appearance; he was half inclined to rush from the place with fear, when he remembered the words of the royal command: "Stay away at your peril."

Presently, the Queen herself appeared, and told him how glad she was that he had come just as he was.

She issued the decree that the beggar should be suitably clothed, and be made one of the princes of her court.

She added, "I told you to come as you were. It seemed to be a strange command to you, but I am glad you have obeyed, and so come."

This is what Jesus Christ says to every creature under heaven. The Gospel invitation is like this: "Come, come, come to Christ, just as you are."

You don't have to feel better, or happier, or sadder. Just come as you are.

You don't have to go to a special place to pray. Come to Christ just as you are. Trust in Jesus, just as you are, and He will save you.

You must dare to trust Him. If anybody complains that you are a filthy sinner and unworthy of any attention, reply, "That is true, so I am; but He Himself told me to come."

Sinner, trust in Jesus. It is impossible to perish while trusting in him. Nothing and no one can pluck you out of His hand. Come to Jesus, and He will not throw you away.

There is no possible reason for Jesus to throw out any sinner who comes to Him.

There is no reason that anyone can think of that will cause Jesus Christ to act in this way. For Christ says "Come to me, all who labour, and are heavy laden, and I will give you rest" (Matthew 11:28).